Curious George®

Big Book
of Adventures

Houghton Mifflin Harcourt
Boston New York

Curious George: The Kite © 2007 Universal Studios
Curious George: The Boat Show © 2008 Universal Studios
Curious George: Roller Coaster © 2007 Universal Studios
Curious George Takes a Trip © 2007 Universal Studios
Curious George: The Dog Show © 2007 Universal Studios
Curious George Plays Mini Golf © 2008 Universal Studios
Curious George: Piñata Party © 2009 Universal Studios
Curious George: A Winter's Nap © 2010 Universal Studios
Curious George: Race Day © 2010 Universal Studios
Curious George: Dinosaur Tracks © 2011 Universal Studios
Curious George: Home Run © 2012 Universal Studios
Curious George: Librarian for a Day © 2012 Universal Studios

For information about permission to reproduce selections from this book, write to Permissions, Houghton Mifflin Harcourt Publishing Company, 215 Park Avenue South, New York, New York 10003.

ISBN: 978-0-544-08463-6

www.hmhco.com

Manufactured in the United States of America
DOC 10 9 8 7 6 5 4 3 2
4500522932

Contents

Niema Jeffers

1................Curious George: The Kite

25................Curious George: The Boat Show

49................Curious George: Roller Coaster

73................Curious George Takes a Trip

97................Curious George: The Dog Show

121................Curious George Plays Mini Golf

145................Curious George: Piñata Party

169................Curious George: A Winter's Nap

193................Curious George: Race Day

219................Curious George: Dinosaur Tracks

243................Curious George: Home Run

269................Curious George: Librarian for a Day

Curious George®

The Kite

Adaptation by Monica Perez
Based on the TV series teleplay written by Joe Fallon

AGES	GRADES	GUIDED READING LEVEL	READING RECOVERY LEVEL	LEXILE® LEVEL
5–7	1–2	I	15–16	370L

It was a sunny day in the country.
George opened the window to let in
fresh cool air.

It was windy.

George liked to watch the wind
carry things away.

It carried leaves away.

It carried his cards away.

It did *not* carry his brick away.

As George looked up,
he saw something colorful in the sky.
It was a kite!

It belonged to Bill, the boy next door.
George wanted to fly the kite more
than anything in the world.

"Flying a kite is not easy," Bill said.
"But I can teach you."
Just then, his mom called,
"Billy, please come and help me!"
Bill gave George the kite string.
"Please watch my kite for me, George,"
he said. "I will be back soon."

George wanted to be good,
but he was also very curious.
He was curious about flying a kite.
George went to a field.
He held the kite up in the wind.
It began to fly away.

George chased the kite.

He chased it over a hill and past a farm.

The string pulled him along.

The wind was too strong.
It carried George away with the kite!

George was flying like a bird.

It was so much fun.

It was fun until George almost crashed
into a tree.

Now Jumpy the squirrel was flying too.
He did not like it.

Soon George was happy to see
the man with the yellow hat
flying nearby.
The man had a yellow hang glider.
He had come to take George
and Jumpy home.

George was glad to be on the
ground again.

He gave Bill the kite.

"Thanks. You are a great kite flyer!"
Bill said.

George liked flying, but he liked
walking more.

George still likes windy days.
He likes to fly kites.

He likes to fly kites that are
just the right size.

BUILD IT YOURSELF!

Here is how *you* can make a
paper airplane of your own.

1. Fold a piece of paper in half the tall way, then unfold it again.

2. Fold down the top corners as shown in the picture.

3. Fold the edges in toward the crease you made in the middle.

4. Now fold the plane in half and turn it to the side.

5. Make a wing from the front of the plane all the way to the back as shown in the picture.

6. You have a paper airplane!

HIGH-FLYING FUN
HOW TO FLY A KITE:

1. Fly on a day that's nicely windy. Check your local weather station—winds of 5-20 mph are best.

2. Face the direction the wind is blowing. Hold your kite straight up in the air and let the wind carry it aloft. Walk and let your line out to help the kite go higher.

3. If you have a friend with you, the friend can stand a few feet away from you and hold the kite. When your friend lets go, you can pull the string in slowly until your kite rises into the air.

4. When you're tired of flying, bring your kite down by reeling in the string and winding it around your kite spool.

DON'T
 . . . fly near telephone wires, trees, airports, or roads.
 . . . fly in rain or electrical storms.
 . . . forget to wear protective hand gear, like leather gloves.
 . . . fly near others.

DO
 . . . fly in an open field, as flat as possible.
 . . . take extra string, in case of mishaps.
 . . . add a colorful tail to your kite. It makes it easier to fly and looks great too.

Have fun!

Curious George®

The Boat Show

Adaptation by Kate O'Sullivan
Based on the TV series teleplay
written by Raye Lankford

AGES	GRADES	GUIDED READING LEVEL	READING RECOVERY LEVEL	LEXILE ® LEVEL
5–7	1–2	I	15–16	380L

It was a beautiful day and
George was curious.
He was curious about all the
boats on the river.

George liked one boat best of all.
It was carrying cars!
"That is a ferryboat," said the man
with the yellow hat.

George liked to boat watch but
he was eager to get to the lake.
If he was lucky, he might see
another ferryboat.

At the lake
there were lots of people.
They were watching the model
boat contest.
There were boats of all kinds.

Bill showed George his model
sailboat.
George thought it was wonderful.

"I saved a lot of
money to build this boat," Bill said.
"Will you keep it safe until the
contest?"

George was happy to help.
He held the boat very carefully.

He looked at the boat.
He looked at his toy cars.
George had an idea.

George made Bill's boat look
just like a ferryboat.

Oh, no!
It sank.
What would Bill enter into the contest now?

George tried to make another
boat for Bill out of his toys.
It sank, too.
George saw that some of the
toys floated.
He had a better idea.

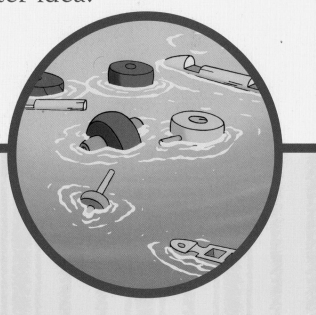

George looked at other boats
on the river.
He made plans to build a boat
from his floating toys.
Bill would be proud.

When Bill came back, he saw the
new boat.
"That is a great ferryboat!" Bill said.

Then George showed Bill what
had happened to the sailboat.

"Uh-oh!" Bill said.
"I forgot to shut the boat's windows.
I'll fix that.

Now water cannot get inside and
the boat will float.
Let's go enter our boats in the
contest!"

Everyone won a blue ribbon for
all their hard work—even George.

Ships Ahoy!

Make a paper boat.

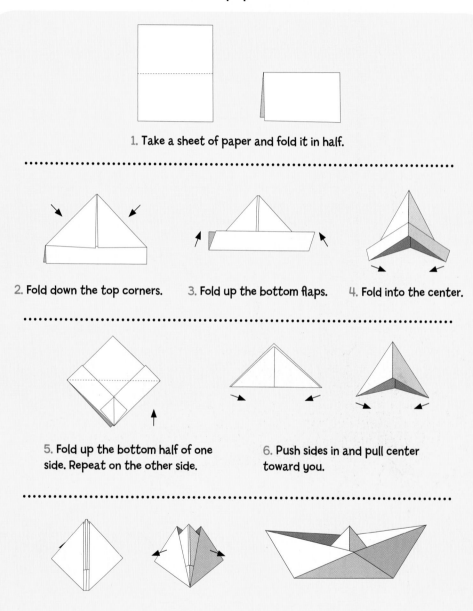

1. Take a sheet of paper and fold it in half.

2. Fold down the top corners.

3. Fold up the bottom flaps.

4. Fold into the center.

5. Fold up the bottom half of one side. Repeat on the other side.

6. Push sides in and pull center toward you.

7. Pull sides away from each other to make your boat!

Now test your boat and see if it floats.

Curious George ®

Roller Coaster

Adaptation by Monica Perez
Based on the TV series teleplay
written by Lazar Saric

AGES	GRADES	GUIDED READING LEVEL	READING RECOVERY LEVEL	LEXILE ® LEVEL
5–7	1–2	J	17	390L

George woke his friend up early.

Today was a special day.

They were going to Zany Island!

George was curious about riding the
roller coaster.
It was called the Turbo Python 3000.

It looked scary and fun.

Betsy and Steve had ridden it nine times!

They invited George to ride with them.
But there was a problem.
George was too short.

The man at the gate said George needed
to be five candy strings tall to ride.
George was only four.

How could George grow one candy
string in a day?
Maybe he could eat leaves like a giraffe.
Giraffes were tall.

Yuck!

The leaves tasted bad.

George took a bite of his candy string.

Candy tasted better.

What else could
he do to grow?
George thought exercising might help.
He lifted a heavy bar.

Then George measured himself.
He was now four and a half
candy strings tall!

George wondered if stretching
would make him grow.
He tried it.
By this time George was very tired.
He nibbled on his candy some more.

George saw a mother and baby.
The mother told the baby that sleep
would help him grow.
So George took a nap too.

When he woke,
he measured again.
Hooray! He was finally five candy
strings tall.

But the sign said he was still too
short to ride.
How could that be?

"Have you been biting your candy
strings, George?" the man with the
yellow hat asked.
George nodded.

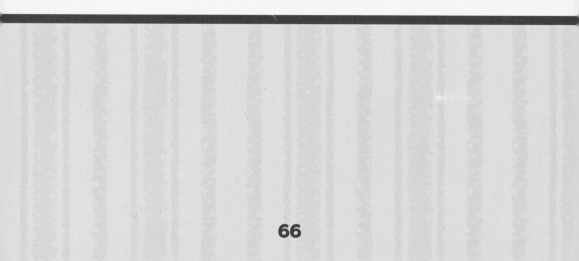

"When the candy strings were longer, it took four to measure you," the man explained.

"Now that the candy strings are shorter, it takes more of them to measure you—five.

But you did not grow."

George was so disappointed.
Captain Zany, the park owner, walked by.
When he heard about George's problem,
he smiled.
"Since monkeys don't grow very tall,
we have a special sign for them."

Was George tall enough now?
You bet he was!

Chart Your Height

Start with a very long sheet of butcher paper or cut open some paper grocery bags and tape them together. Take a ruler or yardstick and draw a line down the edge of the longest side of the paper. Mark off inches all the way up the line.

Decorate your chart with paints, markers, crayons, or stickers.

Before you hang the chart on a wall, measure two feet up from the ground and mark the wall lightly with pencil. Leave this space empty. Place your chart so that its bottom is at the two-foot mark.

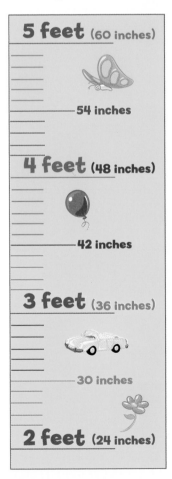

5 feet (60 inches)

54 inches

4 feet (48 inches)

42 inches

3 feet (36 inches)

30 inches

2 feet (24 inches)

Write "two feet" at the bottom of your chart and label every twelfth inch as three feet, four feet, five feet, etc.

Then stand against the chart and have a parent or friend mark your current height with pen or permanent ink on the chart. Label this line with the date and your age. Now when people ask, you can tell them exactly how tall you are!

Every six months, have someone mark your new height. You can probably use this chart for several years. When you are too tall for it, you can take it down, fold it up, and keep it as a record of how fast you grew.

Curious George®

Takes a Trip

Adaptation by Rotem Moscovich
Based on the TV series teleplay
written by Raye Lankford

AGES	GRADES	GUIDED READING LEVEL	READING RECOVERY LEVEL	LEXILE ® LEVEL
5–7	1–2	I	15–16	240L

Winter was long, cold, and snowy
in the big city.
George and the man with the
yellow hat were lucky . . .

They were going on vacation!
The suitcases were ready.
The tickets were ready.

George and his friend went to bed early.
Everything was set . . .

except the alarm clock!

"George! We overslept!" the man cried.

George and his friend dressed.

They dashed off to the airport.

"Hawaii, here we come!" the man said.

George was excited.

He had never been on an airplane before.

The man put the suitcases on a cart at the
airport.

"This will make them easier to carry,"
he said.

They rushed
to check in.
George climbed on top of the cart to
see over the ticket counter.

"Here is a gift for you," the ticket
clerk said.
She gave George a toy plane.
His first airplane!

George liked the airport already.

He flew his plane.

It landed on a red suitcase.

"Bad news," the man said.
"Our plane is late because of a big storm.
We have to sit and wait."
George did not mind waiting.

He had a brand-new toy.
But when George looked,
the toy was GONE!
The suitcase was gone!

Then George heard a beeping sound.

A motor cart drove by.

The red suitcase sat on top.

George ran after it.

The suitcase went faster.

George got on the moving sidewalk.

But he was going the wrong way!

George heard a new noise.

Bags were moving on a long belt.

George spotted the red suitcase.

It was getting away.

George followed it.

He looked inside the suitcase.

No toy plane here.

Where should he look next?

Finally, the plane was ready.

But where was George?

"I cannot board the plane," the man said.

"I lost my monkey!"

"You mean George?"
the flight attendant asked.
She pointed at the plane.
George waved. He was on board already.

George and the man walked to their seats.

A nice woman stopped them.

"There you are! Did you lose this?" she said.

She gave George his toy plane.

That airport was a fun place!
There were so many different ways
to get around.
Maybe it was even better than vacation.

ON THE GO!

Balloon-Powered Train/Car:

You will need safety scissors, tape, a straw, a toy car or train, and a balloon.

1. Cut off the lip of the deflated balloon.
2. Cut the straw in half. Stick the straw into the balloon and tape it in place. Be sure to make a tight seal.
3. Tape the straw to the top of a car or train so the straw extends off the end.
4. Blow up the balloon using the straw and seal the balloon by pinching the straw's end.
5. Set the car down on a smooth surface and let it go.

Getting There Is Half the Fun

A great way to take your own trip is to draw your destination and a "road map" to get there on a piece of butcher

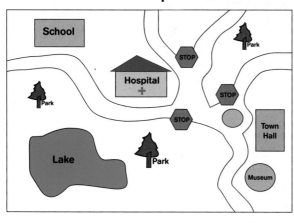

paper. Tear off a section as long as your table. Draw roads, buildings, and street signs. Now you can play with your small cars on your extra-large map!

Curious George ®

The Dog Show

Adaptation by Monica Perez
Based on the TV series teleplay written by Joe Fallon

AGES	GRADES	GUIDED READING LEVEL	READING RECOVERY LEVEL	LEXILE ® LEVEL
5–7	1–2	I	15–16	220L

George was going to a dog show.
He had not been to a dog show before.
He was very curious.

The dog show was a surprise.
The dogs were not doing tricks.
They stood.

They walked.
They ran a little.
That was all.

George visited the dogs after the show.
It was much more fun.

George loved them so much that he
wanted to take them home.

So he did. The dog owners were
busy getting ribbons.

They did not see George leave with
their dogs.

At home George wanted to count
how many new friends he had.
It was hard work!
The dogs did not stay in one place.
George had an idea.

He put the big dogs in one room.

He put the small dogs in another room.

He put the hairy dogs in the bathroom.
Then he counted.
One . . . two . . . three hairy dogs.

One . . . two . . . three small dogs.

One . . . two . . . three big dogs.

The front door opened.
It was George's best friend.

The man was surprised to see dogs behind every door.

"There must be twenty of them!" he said.

But George knew better.
There were three plus three
plus three dogs.
There were nine dogs in all.

The doorbell rang.
Nine dog owners had
come to get their dogs.

George waved goodbye
nine times.
What a great dog show it had been . . .
right in his own home.

rouping numbers is an important math skill. Practice looking at everyday objects with your child and then counting them in different ways. For example, you can group rocks by size or color. Some ideas for counting and grouping: the trees on the playground, the clouds, cars, pens and pencils, pots and pans, and books.

MATCH AND COUNT!

Counting by twos is often faster than counting each item if you have a lot of things to count. Match the socks below and then count the pairs.

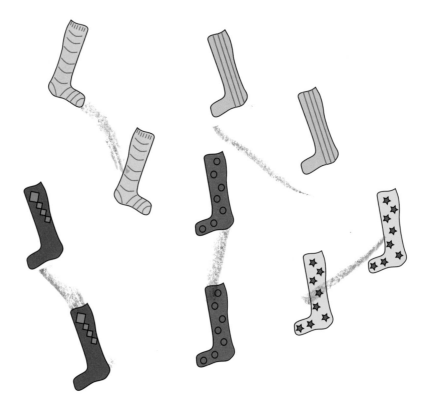

Curious George ®

Plays Mini Golf

Adaptation by Marcy Goldberg Sacks
Based on the TV series teleplay
written by Craig Miller

AGES	GRADES	GUIDED READING LEVEL	READING RECOVERY LEVEL	LEXILE ® LEVEL
5–7	1–2	I	15–16	290L

George and Steve were good friends.
They liked to play games.
Steve always had the high score.
He always won.

One day Steve invited George to
play mini golf.
This was a new game for George.
He was curious.
Maybe he could win this time.

Steve hit the ball one . . . two . . .
three times.
Now it was George's turn.

George took a big swing.
His ball hit two trees!

George swung his golf club
many times to get a high score.

George hit the ball again and again and again.

It went all over the golf course.
Golf was easy!

George hit the ball as many times
as he could.
Finally, he hit it right into the hole.

. At the end of the game, Steve read the scores:
Steve, 35, Betsy, 58, and George . . . 250!

George had the highest score.
He was so happy.
He had won.

"But, George, in golf the *lowest* score is best," Betsy told him. "I won the game," Steve said.

George was surprised.
How could a small number be
better than a big number?

George had an idea.
He wanted to win in golf.
He had to practice.
George asked his friend if he
could borrow some things from
their house.

George made a golf course on the roof!
A paper towel roll was his club.
He blew in one end.
Air came out the other end.

The ball moved.
He was ready to play.
George invited Steve over.

George played first.
He blew through the tube . . .
and got a hole in one!

Steve was next.
But it took him eight tries to get
the ball into the hole.

Steve counted the points.
George had the lowest score.
Finally he was the winner —
of monkey mini golf!

Mini Mini Golf

George used "found objects" to make his own mini golf course. You can do the same using household items like these:

ruler and dry sponge, rubber ball or marbles, paper, tape, scissors, cardboard boxes, paper towel rolls, cotton towels, paper plates, a coffee can, building blocks, or other toys

Instructions:

1. Make a golf club by taping a sponge to the bottom of a ruler.
2. Draw pictures of your ideas for a golf course. Choose one you can build with materials you have.
3. Build your course (see ideas below) using the coffee can as the final hole.
4. Take turns with a friend playing your way through.
5. Talk about what's working and what's not. Do you need to change your design?

Ideas for your golf course:

- Make a tunnel by taping a paper towel roll on the floor.
- Put a chair or stool in the room for your ball to go under.
- Place paper plates on the floor to create obstacles for your ball to go around.
- Make a "sand trap" from a towel.
- Use two rows of building blocks to create a straight pathway.
- Come up with your own creative ideas!

Curious George®

Piñata Party

**Adaptation by Marcy Goldberg Sacks
and Priya Giri Desai
Based on the TV series teleplay
written by Craig Miller**

AGES	GRADES	GUIDED READING LEVEL	READING RECOVERY LEVEL	LEXILE ® LEVEL
5–7	1–2	J	17	230L

George was having fun.
It was Betsy's birthday party.
There were many new things to see
and do.

George heard a wind chime.
He looked up.
A paper animal hung from a tree.
Up close, it smelled sweet.

"That's a piñata," said Betsy.
"There is candy inside."
George had to hit the piñata to get
the candy out.

George wore a blindfold.
He could not see.
He swung, but he kept missing the piñata.

Steve had an idea.

"Practice using your other senses," he said.

"Try to follow Charkie with the blindfold on."

George could not see.
But he could hear.
George followed the barking.

But the city was noisy.
George could not always hear Charkie.
So he used his hands to feel what was
around him.

Click-click.
Charkie's collar made noise.
George followed the sound.
Charkie hid in the fire station.
George felt cold metal.
It was a truck.
He turned on the hose by mistake!
Everything got very wet.

The firefighters turned off the hose.
Now George could smell a wet dog.
He kept chasing Charkie.

Now George felt fur.
Meow! It was his friend Gnocchi.

Mmm . . . George smelled yummy food.
Then he heard Charkie's collar again.

Click-click! George chased Charkie
through the kitchen.

He followed the noisy collar.
Soon there was less city noise.
They were in Endless Park.
George felt wet fur.
He found his doggy friend!

They went back to the party.
George wanted to swing at the
piñata again.

George could not see, so he used his
other senses.
He heard the wind chime in the tree.
He felt the grass under his toes.

He also smelled candy.
George moved to the piñata.
BAM!
Candy flew everywhere.
Now George could use his sense
of TASTE.
That was the best one to use at a
birthday party!

Explore Your World

In the story, George uses his senses to find the piñata. Use your senses in the fun experiments below. You will need an adult to help you put on a blindfold first. Now, no peeking!

SMELL

1. Have an adult place five different foods in separate bowls in from of you. These should be foods that have strong smells, such as garlic, cheese, pickles, and oranges.

2. Lift each bowl up, without touching what is inside, and take a good long sniff.

3. Can you guess which food it is by its odor?

TASTE

1. Have an adult cut up five different foods and place them in separate bowls. These should be foods that have tastes you know, such as grapes, apples, carrots, and cucumbers.

2. Using a fork so you aren't touching the food with your hands, can you guess which foods they are just by tasting them?

3. **Challenge:** Do the same thing with foods you have tasted only once or twice before!

TOUCH

1. Have an adult place five different foods in separate bowls. These should be foods that you can feel and recognize, such as spaghetti, ice cream, uncooked rice, and hard-boiled eggs.

2. Can you guess which foods they are just by touching them?

The next time you go to your favorite park, take a look around you. Where are the trees? Where are the flowers? Make a list of everything you see. Now wear a blindfold, and with the help of a grownup, try to find those things. Use your senses of smell, touch, and hearing to remember where all those objects are. When you're done, take off the blindfold and see how well you did.

Curious George®

A Winter's Nap

Adaptation by Marcy Goldberg Sacks
and Priya Giri Desai
Based on the TV series teleplay
written by Craig Miller

AGES	GRADES	GUIDED READING LEVEL	READING RECOVERY LEVEL	LEXILE® LEVEL
5–7	1–2	H	13–14	430L

One fall day, Bill and George
went fishing.
Bill saw George shivering.
Maybe it was too cold to fish.

On the way home, Bill told George
that some animals, such as bears, go
to sleep when it gets cold.
They eat a lot in the fall.

Then they hibernate,
or sleep, almost all winter. George was
curious. If he hibernated, he would
miss the cold winter months.

At home,
George ate and ate.
Maybe he would get sleepy and
hibernate.

Upstairs in bed, George tried to sleep.
But his room was too bright.

George closed
the curtains.
He painted a picture of the night sky.

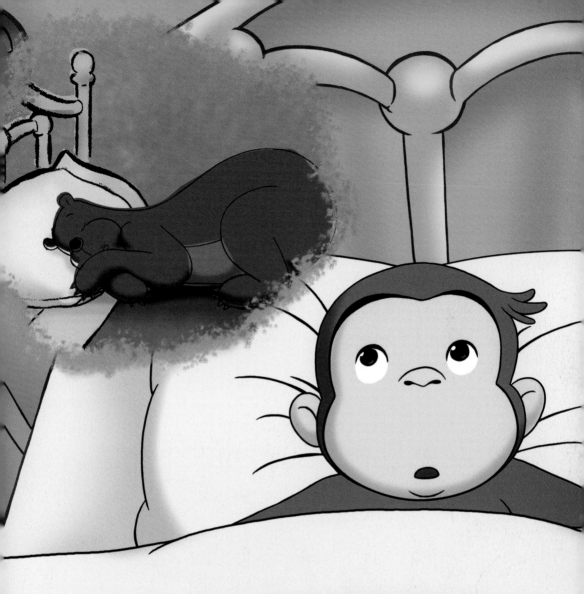

He still could not sleep.
How did bears do it?

George asked the man with the
yellow hat about hibernation.
"This book says bears sleep in
dark, quiet caves," said the man.
That was it!
George needed a cave.

George hung toy bats.
He put rocks in his bed.
Now his room looked like a cave.

George settled in for his long
winter nap.

Uh-oh. Now what?
George could hear sounds outside.

Pigs oinked. Cows mooed.
Chickens clucked.
George shushed them, but they
would not be quiet.

George
covered his ears.
The animals were not as loud.
But his room was not silent yet.

George taped his blanket over
the window.
Now it was dark and quiet.

Finally, George fell asleep.
He slept in his monkey cave
just like a bear.

After a long time, George woke up.
He had done it!
He had hibernated.

"How did you sleep last night?"
asked the man.
Last night! George had slept only
one night, not all winter?
George was sad.
Then the man had an idea.
He took out a box of winter things.

The man reminded George how fun
winter was. They could sled and ski
together.
George did not want to miss winter
after all!

Make a Teddy Bear Cave

Put your favorite teddy bear
or doll to sleep for the winter.
With a few objects from inside
and outside your house, you can
make a cave that is comfortable
to hibernate in all winter long.

1. **Gather materials:**
- A piece of cardboard for the floor of the cave.
- A brown paper bag to create the cave walls.
- A napkin to tuck your bear in.
- Twigs, moss, rocks, and pine needles to make the bed.
- Paints, markers, cotton balls, and anything else you need for decorating.
- A stapler.

2. **Construct your cave:**
- Crumple the paper bag so that you can bend it to make
  the cave walls and ceiling.
- With a grownup's help, staple the bag to the cardboard
  base. Make sure the entrance is large enough to fit your toy.
- Make the bed using the natural objects you found outside.

3. **Decorate your cave like George did:**
- Paint or draw bats on the cave walls.
- Place small rocks around the bed.
- Glue cotton balls around the cave to look like snow.

4. **Now tuck your toy in for his own winter nap!**

Curious George®

Race Day

Adaptation by Samantha McFerrin
Based on the TV series teleplay
written by John Loy

AGES	GRADES	GUIDED READING LEVEL	READING RECOVERY LEVEL	LEXILE® LEVEL
5–7	1–2	J	17	310L

Today, George was helping Professor
Wiseman train for a race.
George had never coached anyone.
It seemed fun and easy.

George started running.
"Wait for me!" said the professor.
She tried to follow George.

But very soon the professor said,
"I'm tired! Can we stop now?"
George was puzzled.
They had barely begun.

George returned home.
The man with the yellow hat
told him not to give up.
He gave George a fitness video.

George watched the video.
He took many notes.
He was ready to coach
Professor Wiseman!

The next day
George used his notes.
First, he and the professor stretched.
Then they ran at a steady pace.

When the professor got thirsty,
George gave her some water.
So far so good!

But Professor Wiseman thought
running was boring.
"I should get back to the museum,"
she said.
George did not understand.
Running was so much fun.
He was curious.
Could he make running fun for
the professor?

The next day, they ran to the Ferris wheel.
"The museum looks so small from up here," said the professor.

Then they ran to more of his
favorite places.
They ran to the puppet show and
to the zoo to see the elephants.

They even ran with balloons!

One day, the professor outran George.
She was ready for the race!

On race day, George and the man
went to the park.
There were so many people there!

"Runners, take your marks!"
The whistle blew, and the runners took off.
George watched the professor as she ran.
It looked like she was having fun!

George wanted to see the
professor cross the finish line.

Suddenly she
stopped running!
George was confused.

Then the professor surprised George. "Will you finish the race with me?" she asked.

George and Professor Wiseman
ran together across the finish line.
She received a medal for finishing
the race.

The professor thanked George for
making exercise fun.
She had another surprise for George.
She wanted him to have her medal!

Having Fun Getting Fit!

In the story, George shows Professor Wiseman that running can be fun. Here's a game to get you jumping like a monkey—you won't even know you're exercising!

HOPSCOTCH

1. Use chalk or masking tape to create a diagram with eight sections. Each player has a marker, such as a stone or button.

2. The first player tosses her marker into the first square. She hops over square one to square two, then continues hopping to square eight and back again. She pauses in square two to pick up her marker, hops in square one, and hops out.

3. All hopping is done on one foot unless two squares are side by side.

4. The rest of the players take their turn, and then everyone continues by tossing his marker into square two.

5. A player is out if he misses a square, steps on a line, puts a foot down, or hops or lands in a square where there is a marker.

Everyday Ways to Stay Healthy!

When you exercise, you work and play hard! But did you know that staying fit is also as easy as closing your eyes?

Exercising makes you tired — **Get plenty of sleep!**
Be sure to recharge your body by sleeping at least eight hours a night.

Exercising makes you sweat — **Drink water before, during, and after!**
You can't play your best if you're thirsty.

Exercising uses energy — **Eat nutritious foods!**
You've heard about superheroes, but have you heard about superfoods? They are foods that pack a nutritious punch, such as avocados, blueberries, fish, sweet potatoes, beans, and oats. They taste good, too.

FLEX A LOUDER MUSCLE!

People can exercise anything from their legs to their arms to their neck to their fingers. Some people, such as singers or public speakers, even exercise their voice.

Try these simple vocal warm-up exercises and strengthen your voice, too!

1. Relax your face and jaw.
2. Stick out your tongue in all directions.
3. Make funny faces. Try to use all of the muscles in your face.
4. Make silly noises while shaking out your body or jumping up and down.
5. Yawn a few times.
6. Hum for ten seconds to get your lips and nose tingling.
7. Flap your lips making a "brr" sound.
8. Say "ahh" and let your voice rise and fall.
9. Sing or hum any song that makes you happy.

Curious George ®

Dinosaur Tracks

Adaptation by Julie Tibbott
Based on the TV series teleplay written
by Bruce Akiyama

AGES	GRADES	GUIDED READING LEVEL	READING RECOVERY LEVEL	LEXILE ® LEVEL
5–7	2	J	17	380L

George was curious about animal tracks. He took photos of raccoon, frog, and squirrel tracks.

"Wow!" said Bill.
"You have almost
every local animal except the fawn.
Come on! I'll show you where to find it."

A fawn is a baby deer.
It would make the perfect photo.

Bill took George to the place he saw
the fawn.
"Good luck," he said. "After I finish fixing
the path, I'm going swimming in the lake."

George looked for
fawn tracks.
The first track he found was from
a slithery garter snake.

225

Then he found duck
and frog tracks.
They both have webbed feet.
That must be why they are good swimmers.

George saw that fish do not
leave any tracks!

Then George found the biggest
tracks he had seen yet!
Could the tracks be from a giant
snake with duck feet?
George followed the tracks.

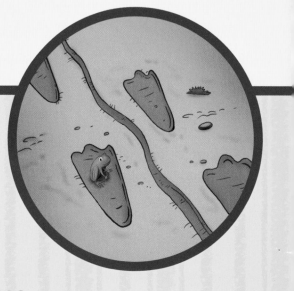

They ended at the
lake. George had an idea.
He had seen these tracks in a book.
They were dinosaur tracks!

He made a trail of food back to his house.
Maybe the dinosaur would come out to eat.
Then George could take a photo.

But wait! George went home to look
at the book.
Some dinosaurs eat meat. Uh-oh.
Maybe they would eat him!

George went
back to the water.
He saw the tracks were now
coming out of the lake!

The tracks were headed toward
Bill's house.
George had to warn Bill!

"I guess those do look like dinosaur
tracks," Bill said.
"But I made the tracks."

"I went swimming with my flippers.
I had my rake too."
George was happy that Bill left the tracks.
A hungry dinosaur would be scary!

George still wanted a special photo.
The trail of food that led to the lake
was still there.

Suddenly, the fawn showed up
to eat the food . . .
with the mama deer!

It was the perfect picture to complete George's collection— even if it was not a dinosaur!

Making Tracks!

Did you know that you can make plaster casts of
animal tracks? Next time you and an adult find an
animal track while on a hike, in a park, or exploring your
own backyard, try it—it's fun and easy!

What you will need:

Plaster of Paris (found at craft stores), a bottle of water, plastic spoons,
paper towels, a plastic container or paper cups to mix the plaster, a small
trowel or something to dig with, paint, a backpack to carry everything in,
and a grownup to help.

What to do:

1. Find a good, clean animal track in mud that has dried enough to keep its shape when you press on it lightly.

2. Lay out all your supplies. Pour about 3/4 cup of plaster into the plastic container. Quickly stir in water until the plaster is thin enough to pour, yet not too runny. Tap on the edge of the container to get out most of the air bubbles. Do this quickly, because the plaster begins to set within a few seconds.

3. Carefully pour the plaster mixture into the track. Let the plaster set for at least a half hour.

4. When the plaster is firm, carefully dig under the cast and lift it up. Take it home and let it dry overnight.

5. When the plaster cast is completely dry, clean it off with a brush. You may want to paint the cast.

Now you have an animal track that will last forever!

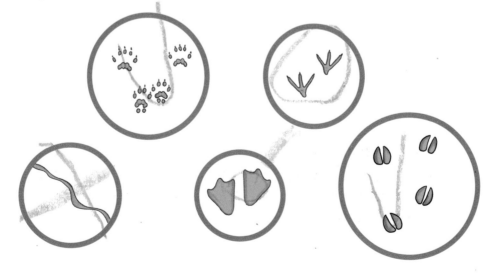

Curious George®

Home Run

Adaptation by Erica Zappy
Based on the TV series teleplay
written by Lazar Saric

AGES	GRADES	GUIDED READING LEVEL	READING RECOVERY LEVEL	LEXILE ® LEVEL
5–7	1–2	I	15–16	460L

Today George was going to his
first baseball game.
His friend Marco was playing.

Marco's team was the Cubby Bears.
They were playing the Tiger Babies.
Marco wanted to hit a home run.
He practiced batting.

Uh-oh.

The scorekeeper was sick.

"Will you help, George?" asked the coach.

Of course! George is always happy to help.

"Every time a team scores, you hang a new number," said Marco. That seemed easy!
But there were lots of numbers.

George waited and waited.
Sometimes baseball moves very slowly!
By the third inning, there were still no
numbers to hang.

Finally, there was some action!
Marco got a hit. His teammate got
one too! Marco slid into home plate
and scored one run.

Now George could put a number on
the scoreboard.
He pulled the number 5 out of the
box and put it up.

"That's the wrong number!" said Marco.
George pulled another number from the
box.
He put up the number 8.

"Use a lower number! You need to put
the numbers up in order," said Marco.
Order? What did that mean?
George was curious.

Marco showed George how to put the
numbers in order.
"Like this: 1, 2, 3, 4, 5, 6, 7, 8, 9, and 10.
Now you try," said Marco.

George practiced putting the numbers
in order.
It worked! He kept score until the game
was tied at 4–4.

George heard a lot of noise
coming from the snack counter.
He could help hand out snacks.

George handed out the food order for number 17.

Then 14.

"Wait," a customer said.

"The number 14 comes before 17!"

"Yeah! And 12 comes before 13!" exclaimed another.

George was confused.
"Do you know your numbers?" the girl
at the snack bar asked.
He counted on his fingers from 1 to 10.

"Here's how to find out what comes after 10," she said. She held her hand over the 1 in the number 11 and the 1 in the number 12.

Now George knew that 11 comes before 12, just like 1 comes before 2. He gave the customers their snacks in order.

When George returned to the game,
Marco was at bat.
But he had hurt his foot.
George would run the bases for Marco!

If Marco got three strikes,
he would get an out.
Strike one! Strike two!

Crack!
Marco hit
the ball hard!
George had to run *very* fast.

George made it around the bases! It
was Marco's first home run. George
was happy to change the scoreboard.
The Cubby Bears had won 5–4!

Rules of the Game

Here are some basic baseball facts.

- **2** teams play against each other.
- There are always **9** players on the field:
    - A pitcher
    - A catcher
    - Players at first, second, and third base
    - Players in left field, right field, and centerfield
    - A shortstop
- There are **9 innings** in a baseball game.
- The winning team is the one that has scored the most runs at the end of nine innings.
- A team scores a run when a player crosses **home plate**.
- Each team has **3 outs** per inning.
- An out is made when
    - a batter gets **3 strikes** (a strike means the batter swung the bat but missed the ball!);
    - a player in the field catches a hit ball before it touches the ground;
    - or a player does not get to the next base before the ball does.

There are other ways to make an out, but these are the most common!

- There are **3 bases** on a baseball field, plus home plate.
- If a batter hits the ball and makes it to first base, that is called a **single**.
- If a batter hits the ball and makes it to second base, that is a **double**.
- When the batter hits the ball and makes it to third base after a hit, that is a **triple**.
- You might already know what happens if a player hits the ball far enough away (usually right out of the park!) to make it to home plate—that's a **home run!**

PLAY BALL!

Keeping Score

Next time you play a game with your friends or watch a baseball game on TV, try to keep score, just like George!

Materials:

- paper
- scissors
- a ruler
- tape
- colored pencils, markers, or crayons

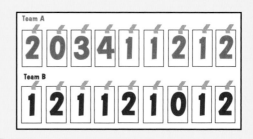

Make your scorecards and scoreboard:

Before you begin, ask an adult for help.

1. Cut out twenty small paper rectangles.

2. Separate them into two piles of ten.

3. Using a colored pencil or marker, label one of the piles 1 through 10.

4. Repeat with the second pile, using a different color for the other team.

5. Use one large sheet of paper as your scoreboard. On the top left-hand side, write the one team name. Halfway down the paper on the left side, write the other team name.

6. Keep score by taping the card with the number of runs that each team has next to the name on the scoreboard.

7. Save the score cards and scoreboard and use them again!

Curious George®

Librarian for a Day

Adaptation by Julie Tibbott
Based on the TV series teleplay written by Scott Gray

AGES	GRADES	GUIDED READING LEVEL	READING RECOVERY LEVEL	LEXILE ® LEVEL
5–7	2	J	17	480L

George goes to the library once a week.
This time the librarian, Mrs. Dewey,
asked George to help her.

Mrs. Dewey gave George a cart.
It held books and DVDs.
George had to sort them into two piles.
George was super fast!

Then Mrs. Dewey
had to leave in a hurry. Her
book club needed her. She put
George in charge of the library!

George wondered. Should he put
the books away?
It seemed like something a
monkey in charge would do.

George put the books away in
record time.
This librarian stuff was easy.

Then the doorman came into the library.
"Hi, George," said the doorman. "Can you
help me find my dog Hundley's favorite
book? It's a yellow book."

George was very
familiar with that color.
The yellow books George found
were not the right ones.
There were a lot of yellow books!

Finally, George found the right book. "Thanks, George!" said the doorman.

Finding books was
hard! George was curious.
Would the books be easier to find if
they were sorted by color?

After George sorted the books, Chef Pisghetti came in.
"I can't find my cat Gnocchi's favorite book, *Mice Everywhere*," he said.

George just needed
to know what color the book was.
The chef didn't know the book's color.
He did know that it was very, very big!

George looked for a big book.
There were big books in every color!
At last, George found the right one.
It was heavy.
"Thanks, George," said the chef.

George decided to try putting the
books in order of size: little books,
medium books, big books.
George had fixed the library again!

But then Steve needed help too.
"George, the books are all messed up!"
Steve said. "This is where all the outer
space books are supposed to be."

George showed how he had sorted the books by size.

"I don't think that's how libraries work," Steve said.

He showed George where all of the books about outer space were supposed to be.

This made George even more curious.

George wondered: If all the outer space books go together, maybe books are organized by subject. Steve said the subject is what the book is about.

George needed to fix the library
again before Mrs. Dewey came back.
Steve helped George sort the books
by subject.

"It's neat as a pin in here!" Mrs. Dewey said when she returned. She explained that books are arranged by subject, and then alphabetically by the author's last name.

Alphabetically means in the same order as the letters of the alphabet.
Names that start with the letter A come before names that start with B.
And names that start with Z go last.
Z is the last letter of the alphabet.

George had had fun helping at the
library.
But he was happy to go home with his
own favorite book!

Color and Size Scavenger Hunt!

You and a friend can learn about sorting just like George did!

- **Pick a color with your friend.**

- **Together, find five items of that color. For example, if you picked the color green, you might find a blade of grass, a green apple, a green toy, a green sock, or a green cup. Make sure a grownup has given you permission to collect the items for your scavenger hunt!**

- **Let one person organize the items by size, biggest to smallest.**

- **Now let the other person put the items in alphabetical order, from A to Z. Do you have any items that begin with the letter A? Now you've learned to organize, just like George!**

One of these is not like the others!

George learned that library books are organized by subject. That means books that are about the same thing go together. Look at the rows of pictures below. Each row shows three items that are similar and one that is different. Try to pick out the picture that does not belong. What do the other three items have in common?

Row 1: The man with the yellow hat; row 2: flowers; row 3: sailboat; row 4: baseball bat

292